The Tunnellers

Maid Marion's People

By Helen Dennis

God bless
~ Hela 2011

Dedication

'The Tunnellers' is dedicated to my husband Tony, our children Jessica, Lucy and Tom (who grew up in Maid Marion's Cottage) and to our grandson Elliott.

Acknowledgements

Thank you to those who have helped proof read the book and encouraged me along the way including Liz R, Luke, Liam, Naomi, Jane, Georgie, Beccy, Darcie, Charlotte and Ava.

Thank you to Blidworth Oaks Primary School for holding the first reading at their school and to Blidworth Library for hosting the first book signing.

Thank you to Abbey Gates Primary School at Ravenshead. Pupils produced drawings in a Book Week 2013 competition. The winners featured are: Cameron Staley, Emily Ball, Beth Carley-Jones, Callum Webb, Isabelle Arrell, Rosie Kibble, Elliot Burton, Aimee-Leah Sladen, James Farr & Emma Wakefield.

Mostly I thank God for the wonderful gifts he gives us all, including the gift of family and friends.

www.facebook.com/TheTunnellers

Published by Helen Dennis

Copyright © Helen Dennis 2013

ISBN 978-0-9926063-1-2

*10% of author's profits will go to **Childline 08001111***

The Tunnellers

Maid Marion's People

By Helen Dennis

Introduction – Show and Tell

"So you see it isn't true! It's *only* a silly fairy tale –
like the tooth fairy, but at least she leaves you some
money." Nat said and the whole class burst out
laughing. I went bright red and felt really
embarrassed.

Nottinghamshire's history was the subject for this
week's show and tell. I talked about the things that
proved the tales of Robin Hood and Maid Marion
and Nat explained why she thought it was just a
legend.

I showed the class local history books, which talked
about old cellars and secret tunnels leading to the
church. I showed them things from Maid Marion's
time and before, which my Dad had found with his
metal detector. I spoke about the rumours of hidden
treasure.

Nat's mum wrote for the local paper though and
gave Nat lots of facts and figures to disprove the
legend and the class believed her. It didn't help that

we lived in Maid Marion's Cottage as Nat made more fun of me about this.

I got teased by the other children too, even though our teachers had taken us to see Will Scarlett's grave in our churchyard and we had all been on a school trip to the Major Oak in Sherwood Forest.

I was so fed up as I knew I had to put up with Natalie in the summer holidays as Mum had offered to child-mind for her and her brother George.

Next week's show and tell was about the local coal mines. I wasn't putting my hand up this time, even though Dad worked at the pit until he lost his job last year. Dad took up metal detecting to keep busy until he found work as a delivery driver. I dreamed of what we could do if he found real treasure. Mum wouldn't need to work nights at the hospital; we could go on holiday, move to a big house, I could have my own room and maybe even a puppy. Although I knew Mum's answer would be, *'never,'* to a puppy.

Dad often told us what it was like working down the pit and how some men were nervous as they thought they could hear children laughing and smell food cooking. They had convinced themselves that the pit was haunted. There was *no way* that I was going to do that show and tell!

Chapter 1

The Den

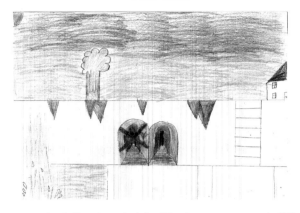

As we sat at the tea table Dad announced: "The summer holidays are only two weeks away so we were thinking of going away for a week to the seaside but ..."

"Oh, please Dad, let's go!" Sam interrupted.

"But, instead we thought we would look at having another bedroom built on so you two don't have to share anymore," Dad said.

"Can it be mine?" Sam jumped in.

"No! *Me – please.*" I begged.

"We'll draw straws for the new bedroom. You never know, Mum and I might end up in there," Dad said.

"But first we need to check if the cellars really do exist, to make sure we can build over them," Mum added, " so, eat up, as the builder is coming in half an hour."

I had been very happy when our 'surprise' baby brother Jack was born two years earlier. The plan was that the boys would share a room, but Jack kept Sam awake. I wasn't so happy when Sam was moved in to my room – neither was Sam. He was going to secondary school after the summer holidays and I only had one more year at primary school – sharing a bedroom with my brother was embarrassing.

We watched from the window as the builder jumped up and down on the patio, sending Jack into fits of giggles. "It sounds hollow, there's something under here all right," he said, then he got his crow bar, lifted a slab up and started digging.

"Suppose they find treasure!" I said to Sam.

"More like spiders and mice," he replied, and I shuddered.

The builder hammered a metal stake into the patio when suddenly his stake flew through the hole and a '*clunk*' was heard.

"Well, you've lost your tool now – that must have gone down six foot!" Dad declared.

"Oh dear! Now what?" Mum gasped.

"We may as well find out what we are up against," the builder suggested.

We scurried back inside and whilst Jack played in his pram we huddled near the window to watch as the builder dug. Dad then fetched his ladder and a torch and we looked on as the builder, then Dad, disappeared under the patio. The builder declared it was "as safe as houses," so Mum eventually let Sam and I go down too.

After being in the warm sunshine it took a while for my eyes to adapt to the dark, cool cellars but as I stepped off the last rung of the ladder and put my feet on the gritty uneven floor I could see that one red brick arch led to another. The smell of fresh earth was followed by a dusty, damp smell. Sam rushed from one archway to another whilst I carefully looked around each cellar.

 I ran my hand over a cold stone slab and Dad said: "That's where they would have chopped the meat. The blood would drain into a hole underneath - and look that's where they would hang the meat." He pointed to big hooks in the ceiling over the slab. I crossed my arms tightly. Dad put the torch under his chin and chased us around the cellar. I pretended to be brave about the blood but there was one thing for sure – with all those cobwebs Sam was definitely right about the spiders! I didn't even want to think about mice! I was up the ladder and out.

Sam nagged Mum and Dad to let us use the cellars as a den (at least until the builders came) and eventually they gave in. I wasn't so keen but I didn't want Sam calling me a 'scaredy-cat' so I went along with it. I was so glad I did as the next few weeks turned out to be the best school holiday adventure anyone could ever wish for.

On Saturday morning Dad, Sam and I swept the cellars, filling lots of bin bags. I found four old coins and Sam found an old knife. Dad bought some big tubs of white paint, so the following weekend we painted the walls and the ceiling and it looked so much friendlier, especially with the cobwebs gone.

We decided that we would make a time capsule with Natalie and George and put the coins and the knife in it, then bury it, for someone to find in the future. I couldn't wait to show Natalie and George the den and, even though she had teased me about our house, I knew she would enjoy making the time capsule. I phoned her to tell her to bring photos and anything else to go in it.

On Monday morning I woke up early to pack us all a picnic. Sam took chairs and a table down to the den with a battery run radio, four torches and some games.

George went straight down the ladder to the den but Natalie was a bit sulky to start with. Once she was down there though we got busy making the time capsule. Mum kept appearing at the top of the ladder to check up on us but left us alone in the afternoon once she knew we were alright.

We wrote stories about our lives and put these in the time capsule (which was just an old plastic food box) with some photos of our family. It was a bit sad as their mum was divorced from their dad and he had a new family so they didn't see him much. We also put that day's newspaper in. Natalie's mum said the newspaper was 'timely' as it talked about the local pit being under threat of closure. I put the notes that Nat and I had made (for the show and tell), in the box too.

We had our picnic and the boys started being silly switching the torches off and making ghost sounds: "Woooo," went Sam.

"Woooaaaaaa," added George. Natalie squealed and ran up the ladder to the garden but I persuaded her to come back down to finish the capsule.

"We need to bury it somewhere," Natalie said. "We could take some bricks out of the wall."

"No way," Sam said "Dad has just painted that."

"I know" George said "Let's see if we can lift this stone slab." I shuddered at the thought of all the dry blood that would be under there but decided to be brave and we all pushed and shoved to try to move the slab. It wouldn't budge.

"Home time Natalie and George," Mum shouted from the top of the ladder.

"OOOHHHH" – we all sighed. We would have to wait until tomorrow to bury the capsule.

The next morning, whilst Sam sorted out our picnic, I snuck into Dad's shed to find his crowbar. George arrived with his rucksack full of treats and sweets. By the time we got down to the den we were all ready for a snack so we sat around the table chatting and eating.

"Right, let's give this slab another go," George said. We all shoved and pushed again but it was only when Sam lifted one end with Dad's crowbar that we saw it budge – little by little we managed to slide it to one side. Natalie fetched the big torch and I braced myself for the sight of a trough full of dried blood, but instead the torch lit up a stone spiral stair case which went down and down and down. We all stood in silence.

"Wow!" George exclaimed.

"We've got to tell your mum," Natalie said as she turned towards the ladder.

I grabbed her arm and pleaded, "Wait Nat. We could just put the time capsule in and cover it back over OR we can tell Mum and she will make us cover it back over OR we can carefully go down, see what's there, come back and then cover it over."

"We can't go down there!" Natalie protested.

George was getting impatient: "Look Nat, you stand guard up here and we'll go down and you can finish decorating the capsule." She looked worried but agreed. There was no way I was going to sit there whilst the boys had all the fun though.

"Nat, you've got the radio and the big torch, we'll only be a few minutes. We'll be alright," I reassured Nat and myself.

"Don't tell," George said as he disappeared down the steps, and Sam and I followed.

I nervously counted - twenty steps down. My heart was thumping fast. I could hear Natalie very faintly singing along to the radio, *'Every breath you take, every move you make, I'll be watching you.'* It sounded spooky.

Chapter 2

The Pool

We found ourselves in a tunnel, with a door at the other end. . . I could hear trickling water. "What's that?" I asked.

"Shhhh!" Sam insisted

"Come back George," I pleaded as he eagerly ran towards the arched wooden door. I shone my torch around and could see that the tunnel's sides were cut into sandy rocks and the roof was made of old oak beams. The tunnel was as long as a big bus and if you stretched you could touch the moist rock on either side. George jumped up and touched the roof and bits of dust fell down.

"Come on, let's see what's in here." George said as he struggled to turn the round black handle. The door made a creaking noise, and then it flew open. My heart wanted to jump out of my chest as I followed George closely and he nervously whistled: *'Every step you take, I'll be watching you...'*

We followed George through the arched doorway. He stopped whistling. We all stood in silence and something scuttled past our feet. I covered my mouth to stop myself screaming.

"Only a mouse," George announced. There was that shudder again.

"WOW!" Sam exclaimed as we stood in a huge cellar like the ones under our patio. This cellar led into a cave though, and at the end of this cave was a waterfall. A wall of water splashed into what looked like a mini swimming pool then trickled out the other side.

"Fancy a swim?" Sam joked as he jumped from one stepping stone to another to get to the other side. I followed him carefully.

"We only wanted our own bedroom, now we've got a den and a swimming pool!" I announced, as my nerves quickly turned to excitement.

George and Sam hopped back and forth on the stones laughing and joking whilst I sat at the edge of the pool and looked around in amazement.

The stalactites ('think of ballerina legs,' Mum always said) glistened down from the roof of the cave as stalagmites reached up as if trying to point something out. George plonked himself next to me and opened a big bag of sweets.

"We'll have to bring our swimsuits next time," he suggested.

"MMmmm," Sam said as he popped a strawberry chew in his mouth.

"MMmmmm," George copied.

"MMmmm," I joined in.

"MMmmm," came a noise from the cave.

"What was that?" I jumped up.

"Just an echo," George announced.

"Come on we'd better get back," I told them, "We've left Nat too long." I hopped back over the stepping stones and through the door as fast as I could.

"No rush, she'll be fine," Sam said, as we reached the bottom of the steps.

"Oh no I've left my sweets," George said.

"Let's come back tomorrow," Sam suggested. "We can get them then, and remember to sneak your trunks in."

"Okay, I'm not sure if Nat will come down though," George said.

As we got to the top of the steps, I could see that Natalie was not there. Had she followed us and got lost? I ran up the ladder, across the garden and into the kitchen where Nat was with Jack– phew!

"Kate, Natalie says she is bored with the den– come and keep her company," Mum requested.

"Okay," I said. "Thanks Natalie – for not telling Mum," I whispered to her as Mum took Jack up for his nap. "It's amazing down there – you should come with us tomorrow – there's ....."

"I don't want to know!" Nat interrupted. "You left me for ages and there were spiders and a mouse!"

"Oh I'm sorry," I said. Surely that mouse hadn't climbed 20 steps? "Come with us tomorrow – you'll see."

"NO!" She shouted and started crying. "I am never going in that den again."

'Oh *great!*' I thought, grumpily, because even though Mum didn't make me spend all my time with Nat she did expect me to be 'polite' - so I would have to fit my fun around her.

"We've put the slab back," Sam whispered. They looked a bit out of puff. I told the boys what Nat had said and we all agreed that if she wasn't going to come with us, we should keep the pool a secret as she may tell her mum.

That night Sam and I planned how we could get towels down from the airing cupboard and how I would keep my hair dry. Mum's old swimming cap was not my favourite idea so I decided to ask her to plait my hair tightly 'because of the dust in the den.'

"I see you've finished your time capsule," Dad said as he came down the ladder into the den. "We could take some bricks out and bury it in the wall – or lift that slab and bury it under there?"

"NO!" Sam blurted, sliding Dad's crowbar behind one of the brick arches, "I mean, I think the wall is the best idea.

"Yes I agree," I added quickly.

"You are a funny lot. I'll go and get my tools then." Dad said.

"It's alright Dad. You have your tea, we'll all do it together tomorrow." Sam suggested.

"Okay. I do want to look at that slab though - your mum has her eye on it for the hearth," Dad said.

"Oh Dad, leave it for now – we use it as a seat," Sam said as he sat on the slab. Dad smiled and turned to go up the ladder just as the slab wobbled and Sam fell on the floor.

Chapter 3

A Ghost?

I had my swimsuit on under my clothes, Mum had plaited my hair and I had snuck the beach towels out of the airing cupboard and taken them down one by one in my rucksack. The picnic was packed.

"What are you planning to do down there today, now you've finished the time capsule?" Mum asked as she lifted Jack out of his high chair.

"Oh, mmm. We just like being down there – talking and drawing. Mm and .." I said.

"Playing games and having fun," Sam added.

"Well you do need some fresh air and exercise so we will be going to the park today after lunch. Natalie doesn't like the den so she is going to practice her clarinet and help me with Jack," Mum announced as she whisked Jack upstairs to change him. Nat did agree to pretend to bring us drinks though, so that kept Mum away but each day after that we were only allowed the morning in the den.

"Right, let's go," George sensed the urgency. Natalie got her clarinet out and started to practice. Oh no not that song again: *'Every bond you break, every step you take, I'll be watching you.'* We could hear the wobbly notes as we went into the den.

We rushed down the steps, through the tunnel door and quickly piled our clothes on a bench in the dry cellar before jumping on the stepping stones then splashing into the pool. We swam under the waterfall, hiding from each other. The rays from our torches flickered on the surface of the pool as our voices echoed around the cave and the cellar. I couldn't stop laughing when George chased Sam across the stepping stones slipping on the last one and landing upside down in the pool. He pretended to be cross with me for laughing and came after me pulling me under the water by my feet.

We were all getting hungry so we sat in our towels in the cellar. "That's funny," George said, "My sweets aren't here – the ones I left yesterday? Good job Mum has put another pack in though," he laughed as he pulled the bag of strawberry chews out of his rucksack.

"MMmmm," he declared as he popped the chew in his mouth.

"MMmmm," Sam copied.

"MMmmm," I joined in.

"MMmmm," came a noise from the waterfall.

"There it is again!" I jumped up.

"It's just an echo." Sam said.

"Well why didn't that last thing you just asked echo then?" I said nervously.

"ECHO," George shouted.

"ECHO," Sam copied.

"ECHO," I nervously followed. There was a long silence.

"ECHO," came a much louder voice from the waterfall.

"I don't like it; let's go," I said, "we've got to be back for one anyway".

"But it's only half past eleven," George pleaded.

"We'll check behind the waterfall," Sam said, with a nervous wobble in his voice.

"Ok, but we should all take our torches," I said sounding braver than I felt.

We stepped over the stepping stones and climbed up some dry rocks to the side of the waterfall. We somehow managed to get behind the waterfall without getting wet again. It was even more magical looking out through the water and being in a dry tunnel. This one was built in bricks with an arched roof. The boys started their torch tricks again, putting them under their chins and pulling faces shouting, "WOOOooo!"

 Then suddenly George stopped laughing and stood perfectly still and silent.

"Don't George," I pleaded.

"L ...I ...I ...look," he whispered pointing to a big rock in the opposite corner.

"What now?" Sam despaired, but then stood totally still and silent too.

"Look, I'm going to stay with Nat tomorrow if you two carry on like this," I said as I shone my torch onto the rock, then joined them in stillness and silence.

Two big eyes stared back at us over the top of the rock. "WOOOooo," came a voice and we all fell backwards dropping our torches. A long chuckle rolled over the rock and I could tell this was another boy - but what was he doing down here?

The big eyes belonged to a very round face which had shiny cheeks and a turned up nose -all framed by tight curls. "Hello. I be Philip – they do call me Pip though. Who be you?" It wasn't cold but we were all shaking.

"I be - I mean I am George," George bravely replied. "This is Kate and this is Sam."

"Why you be here?" Pip asked.

"Uurgh, umm, we've been playing – this is part of our den," Sam tried to sound as brave as George, "But why are *you* here?"

"I do live 'ere," protested Pip coming out from behind the rock and standing up with his chest pushed out proudly. I giggled nervously at his clothes which looked like they were made out of sack.

"What be them?" • ℮ asked as he pointed to the bag of sweets. I hadn't found my voice yet but pushed the bag towards him. Pip sat down next to me and opened one of the sweets: "MMmmm."

'Mmm indeed,' I thought – I bet he ate the bag left by George yesterday.

"Where you be living? Are you from the Up People?" Pip asked. I laughed nervously as it sounded like a pop group.

"We live in a cottage – up the steps," at last my voice came out. "Where do you live? I haven't seen you in our village. Do you have a cottage with steps and a den like ours? Is that how you got down here?"

"I can't say. I not be allowed up the steps. I not be allowed here really but I did hear you all laughing. None of us be allowed this far," Pip said. Then there was a scuttling noise coming from behind him and as it got louder and closer, a howling sound filled the cave. It sounded like an old wolf. I was scared. Sam and George stepped back. Pip jumped up and turned around to face the oncoming creature as it leaped on the top of the rock then jumped on top of Pip. We all gasped as he fell to the floor but we were soon relieved to hear him laughing: "Awww - Huw! Huw-dog, get off now. You be showin' me up."

A cute fat puppy with brown floppy ears and a white body with orange and brown patches was licking him all over his face and in his ears. Soon we were all stroking Huw. "He's lovely," I said.

"Pa says he useless. He says he's the daftest dog he ever bred and that he thinks he's human – that be why we call him Huw-dog."

"Flip! Flip!" A little voice could be heard in the distance crying.

"I do have to go now – that be my baby brother. Huw I told you not to leave him. You do come again tomorrow and be bringing some more of those," he said pointing to the sweets as he disappeared behind the rock, "and don't tell no one you did see me."

We sat staring at the space where Pip had been. I got up and shone my torch over the rock. There was a small tunnel right at the back which wound off into the distance. The scuttling noise and Pip's voice, together with the sound of a small child, faded away.

"Now what?" Sam asked leaning over the rock.

"I can't believe it!" George exclaimed, "a boy, like us, down here in our cave?"

"And a puppy - and a child?" Sam added.

"We'd better get back," I remembered reluctantly.

"Let's come back tomorrow," George pleaded, "I will bring as many sweets as he wants." We agreed that we would not tell anyone about Pip, at least until we knew more.

"Your hair looks a bit wet," Mum commented as I walked in the kitchen.

"Oh, um, I wetted it down to keep the dust out," I said.

That night Sam and I lay awake talking about Pip, the puppy and the child. Could they be homeless people who sheltered in there sometimes? Or maybe someone was playing a trick on us? Or was Pip a ghost – maybe the miners were right and these were the ones haunting the pit?

Chapter 4

The Tunnels

The next day we swam, climbed and laughed Pip ate lots of sweets whilst we told him all about our family and about how we had found the den.

He told us that his father was a breeder of beagle dogs which he sold as hunting dogs and that Huw had been part of a litter of 12 pups. His dad had trained the other 11 to hunt in a pack or on their own for hares, rabbits and pheasants but Huw only wanted to play with the children and he howled if he wasn't allowed to.

"Huw helped me find you though– he got your scent and tracked you. He helped me find lots of tunnels and interesting things I might show ye – there be dangers mind so no goin' without me. But Huw - he be no good for hunting and he be greedy too." Pip told us as Huw pounced on the bag of sweets and ran off with it. Pip chased him down the tunnel shouting, "I be off now then."

We had to visit Grandma on Saturday, so we didn't go in the den at all, but George was allowed to sleep over that night. On Sunday Mum insisted that we should come up from the den for lunch, when they would be back from church and when George would be picked up.

We waited by the pool but Pip didn't show up. We decided to go to look for him. We could see a light in the distance as we moved slowly through the tunnel behind the rock. Our breathing seemed very loud but what sounded like a party gradually drowned us out. I could smell Sunday dinner cooking.

At the end of the tunnel and there was a huge rock, similar to the one in our cave. We peered over the top. We were in another cave – it had a small waterfall running into a paddling pool-sized pond at the other end. People of all ages sat around talking, singing and laughing. A man with a very long beard and his hair tied back in what looked like an old rag was playing some sort of guitar. The woman next to him, whose long hair was as red as the flames in their lanterns, sang along whilst Huw sniffed around pinching bits of food from everyone.

They were all dressed in a similar way to Pip – it was like something out of a medieval play. All the women wore beautiful jewellery though - around their necks and wrists. The blue, red and green stones stole light from their fire flamed torches and bounced it back in all sorts of shapes and colours. I wondered if we had wandered into a film set, or a dream. They were too real to be ghosts though.

Everyone was looking down except one boy who looked up at us. I recognised those big eyes and ducked down quickly. We scurried back to our cave and after about ten minutes Pip popped up from behind our rock saying "Don't you be tellin' no one about what you did see down there will ye? It will all be my fault if we be found. It be the Sunday cave ye see. No one work on Sundays," Pip sounded worried. Who was looking for them I thought – were they criminals? They didn't look as if they were.

"But who are these people?" I eventually asked

"They be my village." Pip replied

"Which village?" I wanted to know. "*We* live in Blidworth – this is under us, so which village is it?"

"I not supposed to say – but next time ye be here – so long as not Sunday I will show ye," Pip said.

"We'll come tomorrow," Sam replied and we said goodbye to Pip. On the way back I remembered how Pip had told us that the rumours in our village were true – the tunnels did lead to the St Mary's church. I could remember which way he said too.

"Let's go and see if we can find Jack at church," I said and the boys followed reluctantly. We were soon at a very square door with a round black handle. George pushed and pushed until it opened with that same creaking sound. I could hear the organ and see daylight coming through the church floorboards, which I could touch as this cellar was not very high. We walked around quietly, peeping through the holes in the boards. When the organ stopped I could hear Jack cooing - we were under their pew. Jack dribbled and it dripped through the hole in the floorboards landing on Sam's forehead. We started giggling. Jack heard us, wriggled off Mum's knee and sat looking at the floor. The next thing we knew he was on his tummy and his big brown eyes were looking at us through the hole.

"Tate! Amm!" He shouted.

"Kate and Sam are at home Jack," Mum said as she lifted him up but he wriggled off her lap again and peered through the hole. His little fat fingers tried to reach us. We had our sleeves in our mouths to stop us giggling out loud, and then, when the organ started up, our laughter spluttered out. The people were leaving the church when a sudden rush of wind slammed our tunnel door shut. There was no handle on the inside - we were trapped!

We waited until the church was empty and tried to find a way out through the floor. George found a cellar door and managed to push it hard enough for it to lift up. We scrambled up,into the back of the old church. Someone was just locking the door so we rushed to it shouting, "wait!" The vicar opened the door just as George slammed the trap door shut.

"I didn't see you in the service today," she said.

"We were at the back, sorry," I said as we rushed by the puzzled vicar. We could see Mum and Dad in the car park. We had to get back to put the slab back over the steps. We ran as fast as our legs would take us and we just made it to the table in time for lunch - phew!

Chapter 5

New Friends

The next day Nat had gone to her Grandma's. We told Mum we were going to the park then sneaked back in the side gate. We were soon down the steps.

"Booo!" We all jumped. Pip had ventured to the bottom of our steps.

"I thought you weren't allowed this far?" George said.

"I did come to meet ye and ye not be here. My friends be waitin' to see ye." Pip explained and we all ran towards the pool.

The cave had a magical hazy glow coming from the three children who were huddled around a lantern, next to the pool. "This be Rebecca, this one Hannah and this funny one he my brother Harold," Pip said pointing at them one at a time, I didn't mean to laugh but Harold sounded like such an old name for a little toddler. Harold and Huw were the cause of most of the laughter that day.

"You make my laugh," Harold said pointing at my hair and they all laughed. He jumped with excitement and then, without warning did a head-over-heels. Hannah grabbed him to stop him falling in the pool. "Flip. Flip! ... That did make my cry... I do need a carry," he started to cry and put his hands up to his big brother. His mass of red curls framed a frail, cheeky face with a turned up nose. The same big eyes as his brother's dripped with a few tears, but before long he sat comfortably on Pip's hip. Huw let out a little howl of sympathy and we all laughed, including Harold.

Rebecca and Hannah touched the flowers on my bright t-shirt and leggings. Under their long grey skirts I could see they had leather shoes with crisscross laces up to the knee – a bit like the ballet shoes Mum had bought for me to encourage me to go to classes. These girls were very girly with big brown eyes and long dark hair right down to their bottoms. Rebecca's was straight whilst Hannah's cascaded down in curls. Next they were stroking my tight blonde plaits.

"Why your hair be like this? You be ill?" They asked me.

"I told you you look like a boy, with it like that," Sam teased.

"Get lost!" I replied.

"Pretty," Harold reached over and stroked my plaits.

The boys sat in a circle scratching the ground with stones. "Have you lived in these caves long?" Sam asked.

"I be born here, I will show ye our village," Pip replied.

"We should not show anyone," said Rebecca.

"Mother will punish us if she finds out we 'bin down here even," Hannah protested

"These be our friends, they be good people," Pip replied.

"Yes but they are still Up People," Hannah said.

"I'm sorry but what are Up People?" I asked.

"You. Up- above, you people are. We live down here, you lives up there," Pip said.

"Don't you ever go up – I mean outside?" George enquired.

"Not up. But we do go to Sunshine Valley – I will take ye." Pip said and Hannah frowned. "I will, Hannah – these be friends – we never meet new friends. Anyway, what your village be like?"

"Well it's big – and outside – I mean – up. There are lots of houses and schools and people." Sam replied.

"You can come if you like," I invited Hannah and Rebecca.

"No I won't. Mother would be cross. None of us be allowed up - unless ye is made runner. A runner goes up once a year. Ye have to be 16. We just 11," Pip said pointing to Hannah and Rebecca, who nodded in agreement.

"Why don't we go to *your* village now?" George asked eagerly.

"Alright, but let's have some of them first," Pip was pointing to the sweets, "We don't have them in our village".

Harold squealed when I passed him an opened sweet: "Me do like," he said.

Rebecca led the way through the Sunday cave which was quiet and empty now. "Where is everyone?" I asked as we went down one tunnel then another, left then right. I wished I had thought to leave a trail of bread, like Hansel and Gretel, so we would know our way back but I was sure I could trust Pip. As sure as I could be in what seemed like a dream.

"They all be working – you'll see," Hannah replied. I could see a light in the distance and the tunnel widened the nearer we came to its dazzling brightness.

"Quiet now! Shhh." Pip ordered. Harold, still on Pip's hip, put his fingers on his lips and went "Shhhhhh," which made us all giggle.

"Harold!" Pip scolded him in a whisper and Harold snuggled closer to him. Huw looked up at Pip and let out another howl. "You'd better carry him else he'll give us away," Pip said and I picked Huw up around his warm tummy. Huw licked my ears and I giggled quietly.

I squinted through the bright sunshine. We were high up looking over a narrow green valley, opposite a rock face, which seemed close enough to get to if you were brave enough to take a long run and leap at it. We peered over the huge rocks, which were stopping us falling off the ledge. I could see a stream trickling down a winding path through trees with leaves of all colours on one side, whilst the other side was divided up into squares of land, where people were digging and planting. Plants of all heights and shapes covered most of the soil like a green patchwork. Some children played in the stream whilst others helped with the digging. There were about 40 people working.

"They be growing potatoes, they carrots, they cabbage," Pip pointed out.

"Cabbage – uurgghh," Sam exclaimed and Harold giggled.

"Sshhhh!" Pip insisted. Harold put his finger on his lips and mimed, "Shhh."

"Them be apple trees, them pears and them plums," Pip continued. Then about ten chickens scuttled from under the trees. "That be the cockerel worryin' them. We do keep hens and ducks for eggs. We do sometimes catch hares, rabbits and deer for the cook pot – not with any help from sleepy Huw mind you," Pip said as he ruffled the puppy's head. Huw roused for a minute, then nestled back into my neck. "Over there be Mother and Father. They do grow herbs for medicine and cooking." I recognised them – he was the pony tail man and she had the flame-red hair. "We do grow everything we need here."

I could see a pen with the lots of puppies similar to Huw in it. They had yellow, red, black and brown patches on their white fur."Why isn't Huw with them?" I asked.

"He was a weakling so his ma would not feed him, so I fed him goats' milk with a spoon for the first few days – and then he lapped it up from a dish and hasn't stopped eating since! But the other pups still won't have him," Pip said. Huw's sleepy body was heavy. I thought 'I would *love* to have him.'

"Why is it called Sunshine Valley?" I'm not sure why Sam asked this as the whole area was lit like a stage with sunshine.

"Every village be settled around such narrow crags as these. Ones where Up people can't get in but the sunshine can," Rebecca explained.

"There are more villages like this?" Sam gasped.

"All over England. I will show you our school books next time. Only trouble around here is the Up people's black tunnels are getting very close to ours so we may have to move on," Pip said.

"Black tunnels?" George looked puzzled.

"They mean the coal mines," I said.

"Anyway," Sam said with a smug look on his face, "If we are the Up people you must be the Down people." Pip looked hurt.

"We call ourselves Marion's People, or sometimes, The Tunnellers." Rebecca said. "Let's show them the old book now."

"Our village was started in 1191. I did learn that in school. Hannah and Rebecca's mum be our teacher," Pip said and the girls smiled proudly showing their small white teeth as we set off along a path hidden in the crag side. Hannah's curls flickered with browns and reds in the sun whilst Rebecca's was as black as coal. They both had round cheeks and eye lashes like spiders' legs. Their skin was like the China dolls' my Grandma gave me every Christmas.

"That be where we live," Rebecca pointed to the crag side, which had about 20 caves cut into it with stained glass windows at the front of each, sparkling in the sun, like sweets in a jar. The

Rufford Abbey monks did bring us this glass in the 16th century when their monastery was destroyed. Some came to live here, to help grow food.

"See those huts built on the other side? That be where we make pots and weave baskets? And you see higher up, past the trees they be bee hives them weavers made," Rebecca explained.

Upturned baskets nestled in the crag above the trees like little animals hibernating. "We do collect honey from there – tastes a bit like those sweets – shall we have another one now?" Pip asked as we sat down in what they called, 'The School Cave'.

"This is where we learn to read and write and do mathematics," Hannah explained.

"And we learn about our history and the dangers of the, um – you – um, the Up people," Rebecca added apologetically.

"*And* about new machines *and* the treasure," Pip added excitably.

"SShh," Hannah and Rebecca looked worried.

"What are those little posts over there?" George was not paying attention but looking outside. I had definitely heard Pip say 'treasure'.

"They be where we bury our dead – they have crosses on if you look closer. We did lose my sister Elizabeth last year – she were but six. Lillibut we called her," Pip's eyes watered up.

"How sad," I said and we all stood quietly with tears in our eyes.

 "Mother be having a new baby come Christmas," Pip reassured himself.

"We better take Harold back for his nap," Hannah suggested, so Pip took us back to our cave. As I handed Huw to him he let out a little howl. Tomorrow we would be reunited – and I would find out more about the treasure.

Chapter 6

Treasure?

"Kate, why don't you spend the day with Natalie? She's brought her dolls and hairdressing set," Mum asked the next morning. I did sometimes wish Jack had been born a girl so Mum could have done dolls, hair and ballet properly.

"I will do this afternoon but we are in the middle of a great game in the den. Nat can join us if she likes". I said but I was thinking, *'please say no,'* and thankfully she did.

I was amazed Nat hadn't mentioned the steps to her mum. George told us that she *had* but her mum didn't believe her, told her off for making stories up, then took a long phone call and forgot all about it.

That day Pip whisked us through the tunnels and it all looked a bit more familiar. Before we knew it we were back at The School Cave, where they had classes every afternoon.

"Where is Harold?" I asked Hannah and Rebecca.

"He not well. Sometimes he take ill. That be why he so small." We all sighed at Hannah's reply.

Pip dragged an old chest from the back of the cave. I was sure he would bring the treasure out of here but instead he pulled out a rolled up scroll. "This be our school history papers – the real documents be in our vault cave. Marion Fitzgerald started our village. She be the one who did live in your house – see." Pip showed us a map in old pencil and it said '*Fitzgerald's Manse*,' where our house should be and the map called our village 'Blidworde'. "Though she be rich she did help poor families. She did marry Robyn Hod at Edwinstowe." Pip told us. We all gathered around.

"Maid Marion *did* live in our house then," Sam said.

"At last – proof of the legend!" George exclaimed.

"But ye can't take this nor tell a soul," Pip reminded us. I sighed. We shone our torches on the papers that Hannah laid out on the wooden benches.

*"In this year 1191 I Marion Fitzgerald declare that
safe housing should be provided for the poor and
persecuted of Nottingham in the caves and tunnels
of my aforementioned property in the forest village
of Blidworde. They shall be provided for from my
own estate and the wealth of Robyn Hod of
Scerewod Stod. Each week a messenger shall run
from the safe housing to collect the goods they
cannot grow or make."*

"That be the runner, but read on," Rebecca said

*"Marion and Robyn, keeper of the forest were
wealthy people. It is said of Robyn that he robbed
the rich to feed the poor. They built their first
settlement at Rock Hill in Mansfield where they had
12 houses cut into the sandstone. Their second
settlement at Creswell Crags near Worksop had
caves where many lived. Those residing there
helped build caves, cellars and tunnels through the
cellars beneath Marion's Manse to house other
poor people. One tunnel led to the old wooden
church at the top of the hill - Robyn's men hid their
loot in a cave across the road from this church and
Marion would dress as a boy and go through this
tunnel to the church so she could secretly collect
the treasures from the cave to return to the poor
people. Not once did she get caught.*

"We've been in that tunnel." Sam announced and Pip scowled at him.

"The workers building the settlements and the tunnels found Celtic crosses, Roman coins and brooches, fairy paths and mosaics and other such treasures from Roman times, which they passed to Marion.

"Robyn's men would hide from the King's men in these three communities. Many times they hunted deer in Clunbre and at Rufford Priory in the Dukeries, then they would hide in the Queen Oak, a huge hollow oak tree, sometimes called the Major Oak, in Scerewod Stod.

"King John held Nottingham Castle and spent much time around deer parks at Wollaton, Bestwood and Rainwater. He often stayed at Fountaindale in Rainwater, where Friar Tuck fought Robin at the moat. King John had another castle at Clipstone, where there was a Great Lake of pike and roach. Robyn and his men would fish from this lake by night and bring food to the poor.

"Marion and Robyn married in a church in Edwinstowe and lived to the year 1232 passing on within days of each other. By this time King John reigned and the country was in peril.

45

"Robyn and Marion's last will and testament declared that all their goods and treasures be taken to the tunnel people to secure the future of their village and others like them. They left a document from Richard I pardoning Robyn and his men and gifting land and treasures to the tunnel people 'to secure the future of the country in years to come'. King Richard also signed papers gifting more of his treasure to this village before his death in 1199 together with lands including a large site at Hockerton, in case they ever needed to leave the tunnels. His only condition was that the simple ways be kept for the future, when he could see greed and laziness would rid the main population of the ability to defend themselves or grow or make anything.

"For many centuries these people lived peacefully hunting hare and deer and growing their own foods.

"In the 1300s England was struck with a plague so named The Black Death. Many more joined the tunnel people to escape death for it took one in three lives in every village. Some say the village of Eyham, but a day's ride away, lost its entire people. There followed riots and 'twas then that the Fitzgerald lands were taken and the house destroyed. Forest fires, harsh winters, witchcraft, diseases, wars and all sorts of bad ways took the *peoples of the forests and the lands and it was decreed amongst the tunnel people that no one be allowed up except once a year a strong male, aged over 16 years, may venture up to buy things such as books.*

"The Rock Houses and Creswell Caves were closed and all those remaining there joined the tunnel people. Some loyal to the tunnel people built a worker's cottage on the site of the manse to keep the site secret."

"I went to Eyam on a school trip – it's true the whole village did die. This is amazing – my Dad would love all this," Sam said, and then quickly added, "but I won't tell him."

"Hasn't anyone else ever found you, like we did?" George asked.

"A few, but all were persuaded to keep it secret or they joined us," Hannah replied.

"Who ... who found you?" George asked

"It was 1698 and our ancestors were exploring near Newstead Abbey, where Robin's friend Friar Tuck came from. The King's men had built a tunnel from the Abbey to their hut on the main road. Evil folk had tied a monk up in the tunnel and left him to die so he was rescued and came to live in our village. I suppose The Tunnellers *found him* really. The children made a whistling machine and hung it in the tunnel to frighten those evil folk away. It sounds like a ghost when the wind blows through it, even today," Rebecca laughed.

"In later years Tunneller children found a young man lying down drunk in that same tunnel. He said he was a Lord and a poet and gave them a scroll full of his poems, which be in our vault too," Hannah added. "Some Tunnellers did help in the wars too, when soldiers dug tunnels to hide and store things. We do know all about your history too ye knows."

"That reminds me - let's show them the mole man – he's funny," Hannah suggested as she skipped eagerly down the path.

"Hurry else you'll miss him," Rebecca added.

Pip caught up with us after he had put the school papers and the chest back. We followed the girls through a maze of tunnels this way, that way and down, down, down. I felt dizzy and a little worried as it was so very dark in the cave we ended up in which had black walls made of coal.

"Now ssshhh," ordered Hannah.

"This be funny, just you wait. But be very quiet," Rebecca added.

They tiptoed now and Pip whispered: "This be where we get the black for burning in the winter. This be where the Up People be getting too close to us so we may have to move on."

Rebecca and Hannah led us on to a ledge, pointed to a hole in the wall and then flopped back laughing. "Shhh you'll wake him," Pip whispered.

George, Sam and I all peered through the hole. As we looked down we could see another black cave with someone lying on the floor - a small sooty man with a huge belly which went up and down dramatically with every snore in and every rattling breath out.

"We call him Lazy Larry. Whilst the other men are working he sneaks in here and sleeps," Pip whispered, "we hear them shouting 'Larry! Larry!' And he jumps up, usually bangs his head and goes back through the tunnel at the other side saying 'just a call of nature lads!'" We all giggled and he started to stir.

"Larry!" Came a distant shout and sure enough he rolled over on to his belly and knees, banged his head and scuttled through the tunnel and he really was like a mole. We all laughed out loud when he got his belly stuck in the tunnel and Huw howled. Larry went still, as if he had heard us, then he twitched. He couldn't see as his tummy was filling the entire hole. "Just a call of nature lads!" We heard him shout and he squeezed himself free and scuttled on. We all laughed as Pip did an impression of Lazy Larry scuttling around on the floor with Huw running behind him.

Hannah promised us another adventure on our next visit but told us we needed to be very brave and bring our torches . . .

Chapter 7

Discoveries

On our next visit Pip suggested: "Let's show them father's machine – they won't be using it 'til harvest so no one will be there."

Up, up and up we went this time, through the maze of tunnels. 'Now I know why they call us the Up People' I thought. As we arrived in a huge cave Hannah and Rebecca pulled some sacking off a large wooden structure on wheels. "Stand back," Hannah ordered as Rebecca wound a lever which brought down what looked like eight spiders legs with blades on, spanning out to fill the cave.

"Wow!" George said.

"What *is* that?" Sam asked.

Pip replied: "It be for gathering crops. Father invented it years ago. We don't have room to grow wheat for bread or cereals. Pa designed this to make a tunnel up into a field where it pops up- then they let its legs and blades down, turn it and it sweeps a circle out of the crops, collecting the wheat and grains for us. It is quick as lightening. It then be flipped back up and dropped down the tunnel, which it fills in. Two runners do go on this job – it's amazing and Pa has made six more for other villages like ours and we lend it to the Lincolnshire Tunnellers in return for malt."

"We don't steal though – one of the runners leaves coins in the field for the farmer to find," Rebecca reassured us.

"But where do you get your money?" Sam asked.

"It's the treasure," I told him "that's what all the metal detector people go looking for."

"I wondered how crop circles were made." George said. "It's you! Nobody can work out how all these circles keep appearing and now we know."

"But we can't tell," I reminded him.

Hannah and Rebecca told us tales of Robin Hood's men; Will Scarlett, Little Geste, who was seven-feet tall, and Friar Tuck and how they dressed in 'Lincoln green.' She said they had Robin's sword in their vault tunnel. She told us how they had used these caves and tunnels to hide from the Sheriff. "Robin had a big tunnel built for his fastest horse 'Pancho'. Robin and Pancho would run through the tunnel and under the road to take The Sheriff's men by surprise". I recognised some of the stories she told.

The girls sang a song to us about the Queen of the May and explained this is what Marion was known as and Jack of the Green who was Robin. We laughed and danced together.

"Wait a minute," Sam said. "This is good fun but what about the adventure we needed torches for?" They all jumped up and we followed them as they ran down a different lot of tunnels. Huw ran alongside, sniffing the ground and sometimes falling over his own nose.

"Now grab y'self one of these sacks," Pip ordered. "This is how we move supplies around the tunnels."

"Hold on to it very tightly!" Hannah ordered.

"I'll go first - remember to put your torches on, it's very dark," Rebecca said as she sat on her sack and nudged herself off a small ledge into a tunnel and went whizzing down what looked like a fairground slide. "Weeeeee," her excited cries echoed back up to us.

"Where does it go?" I asked as Pip handed out the sacks and Sam sat on the ledge.

"You'll see – no need to be worryin now – just enjoy the ride," Pip reassured us as my brother disappeared clutching his torch and screaming.

George sat on the ledge then pushed himself off enthusiastically and flew down the slide so quickly that he dropped his torch, which bounced down after him.

"Shall I take Huw?" Hannah offered. I shook my head. I could hear her laughing as she slid out of sight.

"I be going last," Pip said as he pointed me towards the ledge and made sure my torch was on and that Huw was secure in a second sack on my knee. My heart was thumping as I slowly edged off the ledge clutching Huw and my torch tightly. I whirled down the slide, my tummy tickled and I just about managed to stay sitting up. Blue crystals glistened on the roof; small waterfalls ran from one cave to another. Around the corner was a small cave with bars over its entrance. Inside it glistened with reds, golds and what looked like piles of ice – my sack whisked me away before I had chance to take a proper look. I squealed all the way down and landed on my bottom in a load of straw. I couldn't see where Huw was. The others stood laughing at me and when Huw eventually appeared from the straw, still in the sack looking like a ghost dog we all giggled. I jumped up to free him, when suddenly, Pip landed from the slide behind me pushing me back down to the floor and burying Huw again. The little sack gradually reappeared from under the straw howling. He really did look *and sound* like a ghost this time. We all laughed and pulled the sack off him. As we cleaned the straw off our clothes Rebecca led the way down a maze of tunnels and it got darker.

"Look here be the wishing well," Rebecca said as she popped her head into a hole in the side of the tunnel. "*Wishing well*," came the echo. This was a real echo. It seemed to go all the way up to the sky and down to the centre of the earth. We all made our own echo sounds. Huw even howled but when the echoing howl came back he yelped and put his head under my arm.

"C'mon," Pip rushed us and we all ran behind him. Suddenly the tunnel opened up into a cave as big as a church and there was a small lake under its arches, "Wow!" I said and we all stood gazing in silence.

"This be the bottomless lake," Hannah said. "No one can reach the bottom."

"We don't even swim here as it be too deep and Ma says the water is so pure it be made for the angels," Rebecca added.

"But we can go down *here* if you be brave enough?" Pip said pointing to another opening at the side of the church cave. This tunnel had water in it. "This be our underground canal," Pip added as he pulled a small boat with paddles from behind a rock. "This goes for miles but I just be takin' you to one cave today and ye need to be brave."

We all stepped in to the boat not saying if we were brave or not and my heart was thumping. We could touch the damp roof of the tunnel and there was just room at the side of the boat for the paddles, which Hannah and Rebecca used skilfully to move us along the canal. "It only be a few minutes," Rebecca reassured us.

Pip told us stories to pass the time: "Nottingham used to be called The City of Caves but tunnellers no longer live there. Edward the Third used their tunnels though as secret passages to get to

Nottingham Castle to reclaim his throne. He killed a man called Mortimer who had had his father, Edward II, killed with a red hot poker. There be a cave in Nottingham called 'Mortimer's Hole'."

 He told us scary stories about evil highway men who stole from people in Thieveswood between Nottingham and Mansfield. Pip then told us ghost stories about women being burned as people accused them of being witches. Then the boat stopped by an opening into another cave. "And this be the cave where the witches still live!" He said whilst rocking the boat. I felt a shiver down my back as we got out into a much darker cave.

"Be shining your torches over there," Pip said, and as we did a witch's face appeared on the wall. Sam and George let out a shocked sigh and Huw howled, I gasped as the shadow of the witch's hat, nose and chin flickered on the wall.

"Let's go back," I said.

"It's only the shadow from the rock," Sam teased.

Hannah and Rebecca had turned the boat around. Pip started to tell us another story about the witches when Hannah interrupted him: "Shut up now Pip! Tell them about the nice things like our fish ponds." I *was* feeling a bit shivery. Rebecca went on to tell us about blue crystals and special stones that were still being dug out from the sandstone as they built even more tunnels. Hannah added stories of Holy Wells and told us how they dress them in flowers every year to "thank God for the miracle of fresh water." We all settled down and we were soon getting out of the boat.

"How come you don't get caught?" George asked.

"We do only work on new tunnels at night by hand and we very quiet and careful and dig very deep." Pip replied "Mind you our Pa does dress like you sometimes when he goes up to the market once a year to sell honey or the stone we gather and to buy things like coffee and books. He says they call him a 'gypsy traveller.'"

"Pa says the people is as wicked as they ever were and there is so many more of them now. He says most of them don't know how to grow or make anything and they spend most of their time watching other people living their lives in a box – they do call it a 'TV'. Pa is the only one allowed Up – apart from the runner," Pip added.

Pip then got bows and arrows out of a big box. "Girls against boys?" I challenged. We spent ages trying to shoot our arrows at a bag of sweets on the rock – when anyone hit it they got a sweet. Pip won a lot of sweets that day but he let us keep a bow and arrow each.

On another visit Pip and our friends took us deep down to some proper tunnels that had been built in the war by soldiers. These had been used for people to shelter from bombs and to store and move things but were now closed off, unless you were a Tunneller.

We all rode in a wooden trailer along rusty tracks through these very straight tunnels. Hannah and Rebecca pulled ropes, which released water down a big open pipe. This sent the trailer flying up hill and it went even faster downhill. It was a bumpy ride but we laughed and squealed all the way. Then we came to a sudden stop. "Jump out!" Pip ordered and we all followed him through a door and up lots of steps, then through a very narrow tunnel. "Now wait and be very quiet," he said as he slipped sideways through an even tighter space. We all stayed quiet and peered through – we could see people with hard yellow hats on walking through these caves, with cameras.

"These be the Nottingham caves. That tunnel we just came up be Mortimer's," Rebecca said.

"They will be tourists then, Pip will be seen!" I said as one group of tourists moved on and Pip moved quietly towards the display dummy, which was a man bending over working with leather. Pip took a tool from the bench and posed like a dummy. The tour guide had her back to the display as she spoke to the group of Japanese tourists. Just as they were moving on Pip stuck his tongue out and they all chuckled and took photographs, then he slipped back through the narrow gap.

"D'child, he berry funny," one tourist said as he nodded and smiled at the guide, who came back to look at the display. We all held our breath.

"What child?" She asked, but they had all moved on to the next part of the tour. She looked puzzled.

"Pip, they will have your photo now!" I said.

"No matter. If anyone finds out they will think I be a local boy playing about —which I am," Pip said as he ran back down the steps and tunnel and we all followed him and jumped in the cart for the bumpy ride back.

Chapter • •

The Rescue

Mum and Dad were very excited that night as they had booked the builder to come at the end of the school holidays. They couldn't understand our lack of interest. We told them it was because we didn't want to lose the den but really it was all our new friends that we didn't want to lose. Mum had told us that the cellar would be completely filled with rubble and concrete to secure the foundations.

The funny thing was Sam and I hadn't fallen out once since we met Pip and his friends. We were so full of things to talk about at bedtime that it was actually quite good sharing a room.

"Sam – phone for you – it's George – take it up there will you love," Mum passed him the phone on the stairs and I followed him to our room.

"Hello George - she's what? ... Oh no, I'll talk to Kate and ring you back." Sam sounded worried. "Kate, Nat has been moaning to her mum about you not playing with her enough and how she thinks the den isn't safe for George to go in and her mum actually listened this time – she's coming to see Mum in the morning and wants to look in the den! Apparently she wants to write in her newspaper about us finding the cellars. George sounds really upset."

This was my fault – I had got bored that afternoon, so I called her a baby for playing with dolls. She had burst into tears and Mum had told me off.

"We can't have her finding the rest of the story out. We'll have to put the slab back properly and hide the crowbar," Sam said.

That night my legs ached from going up and down through the tunnels and I fell asleep straight away.

At 8am the doorbell rang long and hard. It was Stella, Nat and George's mum. She sat in the kitchen and Mum made her a coffee whilst Jack was in his high chair eating porridge.

"Have you seen the news this morning? It's not hit the papers but I can't stay long as our team want to get it in the evening edition. There's been an accident at the pit - a mine shaft collapsed. They got all but one of the miners out. They are looking for him but apparently the collapse is so bad it looks like it's the end of the pit never mind that poor miner." Stella said. I hoped this was not near Pip and his family.

Jack sneezed and his porridge covered Stella's navy suit like a splatter gun. "OH, No! Now look!" Stella shouted as she tried to wipe it off with kitchen roll. Then her mobile phone rang and she took the call.

"I'm so sorry," Mum said as she tried to remove the porridge blobs.

Stella snapped her phone shut, turned to Nat and said, "Look Natalie you will just have to play nicely with Kate – she is a lovely girl. I will have a quick look at this den but I've got to fly as we've got to get this pit story to print."

Stella, Mum, Nat and I went down into the den whilst Sam and George cleaned Jack up. "It seems fine to me," Stella said as she looked around, "What's under the slab – Nat said something about steps under a slab?"

"I can't budge it," Mum said honestly as she tried to. Stella had a go and broke one of her red painted nails and swore. Stella's high heels stomped up each rung of the ladder, and we all followed her into the kitchen.

"Natalie – you must stop telling tales!" She snapped as she slapped Nat across the leg. Mum winced and I instantly felt sorry for Nat. "I've got to go!" She glared at Natalie.

"Can I still go in the den Mum?" George shouted.

"Yes," she replied curtly and slammed the door behind her. Jack sneezed again and we all laughed except Nat who cried and I felt bad for her again.

"Come in the den with us," I said and I meant it this time.

"I might," she sobbed.

"How awful," Mum shouted from the kitchen. "Look its Mrs Lawrence's husband who is trapped in the pit." His picture was on the breakfast news – it was Lazy Larry!

I pointed to the TV as Sam gasped and blurted out, "Lazy Larry!"

"That's a bit rude Sam – this man could be dead for all we know," Mum replied.

"Sorry Mum," Sam was in the same trance I was in.

"We – we'll be going to the park now Mum," I said.

"Hold it right there," she replied. "You can tidy your room first and I need a bit of help today. After you have done your room Sam you can peg those two loads out for me and Kate you can vacuum through." We worked like lightening. Nat tried to help.

Eventually Mum was happy and we were on our way – out the front gate, in through the side gate and quickly into the den. Nat was right behind me. I decided to be firm with her: "Nat, it's time to be brave. We are going down the steps and you will not believe your eyes. If you come with us you have got to promise not to tell anyone what you see."

"I, I promise," Nat replied. I quickly told her about all the wonderful things we had been doing as we went down the steps. She whimpered a bit when we got to the first cave, then gasped when Pip appeared in the first lot of tunnels but eventually she settled, especially when she met Hannah and Rebecca who were so very gentle and kind to her. Again I felt guilty. They took great interest in the bag of Barbie dolls she had taken down with her.

"It's Lazy Larry," George announced.

"I know," Pip replied "we've got him." Pip led us into the Sunday cave where there was a pile of blankets with Larry's head peeping out.

"Is he OK?" I asked.

"He will be,"said a deep voice from behind the rock. We all jumped. It was Pip and Harold's father. "Now don't you be worryin' none. Pip and these girls should not be showin' you the things here but that be our business. We cannot see a man sufferin' and not help but we do have our own problems so need you to be helpin' too."

Pip told us how Harold had become even more unwell and they were very worried about him so they needed us to help to sort Larry out. Larry had taken a bang to the head and was confused but otherwise seemed alright. Pip's mum had mixed some herbs to keep him sleepy. Larry suddenly sat up. "Just a call of nature lads!" He shouted then collapsed back. We couldn't help but giggle and Pip's dad smiled a big smile and said "I think he needs a top up – I'll send Rose."

Pip's mum came with medicines, holding Harold in her arms. She looked pale. Poor little Harold looked very unwell, clinging onto his mum's neck. He reached over and touched Natalie's brown bob and said "pretty!" We all smiled, including Nat.

Larry was given more herbs and his big belly rose and fell to the sound of his rasping snores. The plan was to use the crop circling machine to make a tunnel into the local park tonight, then pop him out before filling it back in. We arranged to meet them there at midnight.

We had time to show Nat some of the adventures we had been on. Pip even took us to Sunshine Valley. This time we did jump the crags. Pip had some huge swing ropes and we all swung across – even Nat, although she did look a bit pale when she was waiting for her turn. George went after Pip, and showing off to Rebecca and Hannah he beat his chest as he swung across but then lost grip with his other hand. We all gasped. He almost fell but just scrambled over enough for Pip to grab him. We all stood quietly. George turned and took a bow and we all laughed with relief.

We sat at the top of the valley eating our picnic and planning the job we had to do that night, then Pip took us back to the den ready for the evening ahead of us.

Nat and George persuaded their mum to let them stay over. With the pit story to write she hadn't resisted too much. Mum was at work and Dad had Jack in their room at the other end of the house so the boys could go in Jack's room. This meant they wouldn't hear us sneak out later.

Dad was a bit confused that we had all settled to bed so well when he came to say goodnight. "You are a funny lot!" He said as he went downstairs.

We waited until Jack and Dad were in bed. It was a cool night but dry and still. We had made a sort of giant skate board that afternoon out of Jack's old pram. We had taken the carrycot off and tied planks together so we could hopefully roll Larry on to this. We told Mum we would need it for the village parade later that month, which we probably would.

We managed to sneak down the stairs to the front door without a moan from Nat, who was now up for the adventure, but just as we turned the latch on the front door we heard Jack whimper and could hear Dad getting up.

"Have you lost your dummy?" Dad asked Jack.

We stood like musical statues for what seemed like hours but was probably only five minutes before it went quiet again, apart from Dad's soft snoring (Mum always said he sounded as if he was blowing cake candles out).

We quietly opened the door and were off down the street like alley cats – the boys went ahead whilst Nat and I towed the giant skateboard, which we named the 'Larry-mobile'.

"I'm sorry I have been mean," I said to her.

"Me too," she replied.

"C'mon let's run for it," I said and we soon caught up with the boys at the park.

We sat on a bench waiting and wondering how and where the tunnel would appear when suddenly a police car went by with its lights flashing. "I don't believe it!" Sam gasped and we all dropped down behind the bench. We held our breath for ages then all burst out laughing. George offered more strawberry chews around.

"Has your mum got shares in these?" Sam joked.

"No, but she does go out with the man who runs the newspaper shop, where she buys them," Nat replied.

We all laughed again when suddenly, behind the bench, the soil started erupting. We all fell back on the grass and kept shuffling away as the circle got bigger. We sat on the roundabout watching with mouths wide open as the machine disappeared back into the hole. We strained our eyes to see a wobbly head gradually come out of the hole. Then Larry popped out and he rolled onto the grass.

"Don't worry," said a deep voice from the tunnel, "he has just had some more herbs and will be asleep any minute." Larry got to his feet, staggered around, then tripped over the path and landed right on to our Larry-mobile, looking up to the sky. The only thing was he was the wrong way around, lying across it, instead of along it.

The machine reappeared, scooped the earth back down and flattened the ground before disappearing again, leaving only a few flicks of mud. I could hear something scuttling around in the bushes. "Sshhh!" I ordered. A little howl came and I could see Huw's flag tail waving –he had escaped the tunnels and couldn't get back.

"Huw," I shouted, "come here boy!" Huw bounced out of the bushes with his brown ears flapping up and down, jumped on Larry and licked his face then ran to me.

We tried to turn Larry around but every time we tried he woke up a bit and started shouting "Lads, lads," and Huw let out a little howl so we decided to try to move him as he was. Getting out of the park was the tricky bit as we had to bend his legs and arms up so we could fit him through the narrow gate. He let out a huge snort in the middle and once again we were in fits of laughter.

We knew his house was on the next street so, after nearly losing him when we bumped down the pavement, we were confident we could get him there. What we had forgotten was that it was a downhill road and the Larry-mobile got faster and faster until just as we arrived near his house we had to let it go. It bumped into the kerb and threw him on to the path just outside his home. "Lads, lads!" He shouted as he looked straight at us. I could hear another siren. Huw bounced up to Larry, licked his face again, then ran back to me.

"Come on, let's go," I said as I scooped Huw up into my arms and grabbed Nat's hand. Sam and George dragged the cart. We ran home as fast as we could. How we snuck back to bed without Dad hearing us I do not know. How we kept Huw quiet is an even bigger mystery but he seemed to like sleeping in my bed with me.

Chapter 9

Illness

The next morning we all got up early to watch the news on the old TV in our bedroom:

"In a mysterious course of events the miner trapped in Blidworth Colliery has reappeared at his home. Suffering from concussion he consistently claims that a group of young children and a puppy brought him out through some tunnels. Jack Lawrence's wife heard a commotion outside their home just after midnight last night and went out to find her husband on the pavement. Police are investigating his claims although doctors at the hospital where he is recovering say hallucinations are common after a head injury.

"As another blow the Coal Board has announced that they now intend to close this pit and will not be doing any further mining works in this area for the foreseeable future."

"He saw us!" Sam announced.

"Oh this is awful!" Nat said pulling the cushion to her face to hide her tears.

"Good news for Pip though – they won't have to move," I thought, out loud. The phone rang.

"George it's for you – it's your mum," Mum called and George took the phone off her on the stairs.

"We haven't been up to anything Mum..... Of course it's nothing to do with us .... How could it be? We were here all night. .....No we didn't see or hear anything. ....I know it's near but we didn't. ... You said Nat was making that up. Okay, see you later." George hung up. "She knows something's up, she's coming to see your mum after work," he informed us.

"We've got big problems now," Sam announced

"No we haven't," Mum said as she walked in the room with a letter in her hand. I hid Huw under the covers. "The planning permission has come through – much sooner than we thought, so we may be able to get started straight away."

Later that morning we managed to sneak Huw out of the house and back to Pip, who was with Rebecca and Hannah in the Sunday cave. It was so hard to hand Huw back but we were full of excitement about the success of Larry's rescue and couldn't wait to tell them that they didn't need to move the village. But they still looked sad.

"What's the matter?" I asked.

They could not hold their tears back as Pip choked out the words: "It's Harold. Mother did give him all the herbs she can think of but he worse. He dying!"

We all started to cry at this news but after a few minutes George said, "He can't be – he's only two. Surely there is something we can do."

We didn't swim, climb or explore that day – just sat kicking the stones and talking about Harold and about how we would all have to say goodbye sooner than we thought. I held Huw tighter.

Then Nat said, "Your mum is a nurse. She might know what is wrong with Harold."

"But we'd have to tell her everything!" Sam exclaimed.

"What do you think?" George asked Pip, Hannah and Rebecca.

"Well your dad did break the rules to help Larry so he might break them to help Harold," Hannah wisely suggested to Pip.

"Let's go and ask them," Rebecca added.

"What if we just brought Mum down here later – then they couldn't say 'no'?" I asked and it was agreed.

Dad arrived home early and Nat and George were staying for tea as their mum was working late on the pit story.

"Let's draw straws," he said as he excitedly produced a handful of straws. "Whoever gets the shortest straw gets the new room." We all looked quite glum as our minds were elsewhere. "You are a funny lot! What's the matter with you? I thought you would be excited – the builder is coming tomorrow teatime to make a start." We looked even more sad as Sam, Mum, Dad, Jack then me each pulled a straw – it didn't even make us laugh when Jack put his up his nose.

"And Sam gets the room!" Dad announced. Not even Sam looked happy. "There really is something the matter – come on you had better tell us."

"We need your help Mum – and Dad's. It's really serious," I said as I started to cry. They both pushed their plates away and Mum took the straw off Jack (which he was now blowing raspberries through) and replaced it with his dummy.

Just as I was about to start talking there was a knock at the door. It was Stella. George peeped out the window.

"Oh no! She's got a photographer with her," George despaired.

"I'll handle this," Dad said firmly.

"Ah – I've come to collect George and Natalie but Kathy said it would be okay to run an article about the old cellars you found under your house so can we come in please?" Stella was on a mission.

"You'll have to go – quick!" I whispered to Nat and she grabbed her coat. "Don't say a word," I ordered and she nodded her head as she grabbed George's arm.

"Ready Mum," she announced.

"But I need to do this story Nat, go back in!" Stella insisted.

"I'm sorry Stella – we have a bit of a family emergency, so now is not a good time," Dad said ushering them out of the door.

"Perhaps I could just get the pics today?" She persisted.

"No way Dad!" Sam spat the words out.

"I'm sorry Stella – come tomorrow after work and we'll have a coffee," Mum offered.

Stella looked disgruntled as she stomped off with George and Nat walking sheepishly behind her.

"Now what is this all about?" Dad asked.

We told them everything.

"This is all my fault. I'm sorry kids but I think I have given you too much freedom this holiday and your imaginations have run away with you!" Mum announced.

Dad was thoughtful: "Mr Lawrence was very insistent that it was children who saved him."

"Mum we need your help with Harold. He's the same age as our Jack – I know you would want to help him if you saw him." I pleaded. Mum scooped Jack out of his high chair and held him close to her.

"I am going to bath Jack and put him to bed. By the time I come down I hope this will make better sense than it does now." Mum sounded bewildered. We told Dad more about the school and the history books, and how the Tunnellers grew their food, and the crop circles, and how poorly Harold was.

Eventually he said, "Well the only thing to do is to see this with my own eyes."

"Kath, Kathy," he shouted up the stairs, "I am going in the den with the kids." He didn't wait for her reply.

"Wait, we need Mum too. She is the nurse," I said.

Dad rang our baby sitter. She only lived two doors away so by the time Mum reappeared with armfuls of laundry, saying Jack was asleep, the babysitter was at the door and Mum reluctantly agreed to come with us.

"Don't answer the door to anyone," Dad told the sitter. She looked bemused but put the TV on in the front room and sat down. "We've got to check out the extension plans – we won't be long," he added.

"Come on, we need to see this for ourselves Kathy – one way or the other," Dad said and Mum put her trainers on shaking her head.

I led the way and Sam followed behind Dad and Mum. We took them carefully down the steps and walked briskly through the first tunnel.

"Wow," Dad exclaimed when he saw our pool.

"Aren't they our beach towels?" Mum asked.

"This way," I rushed them over the stepping stones and behind the rock to the Sunday cave. I was worried as there was no sign of Pip or anyone. "Come on!" I hurried down the next lot of tunnels, left then right, then right again.

"I'm not sure we will find our way back," Sam shouted.

"We will," I said. I had marked every corner we had turned with a stone

"Look, we're at Sunshine Valley!" Sam announced. Mum and Dad peered over the rock and gasped at the sight of this beautiful village.

"Good grief," Mum said, "It's like something from medieval times!"

I could see Pip coming towards us. "Wait here," I said as Sam and I went to meet Pip. He looked so sad. I hoped we weren't too late.

"He bad – Harold – he really bad," Pip said with tears in his eyes.

"We brought Mum – and Dad. Lazy Larry has been telling everyone about us and although most people don't believe him some are asking questions so we need to move fast." Sam said.

"Mother and Father have said the nurse can see," Pip said. So Mum and I were led into what Pip told us was 'The Hospital Cave,' where Harold was with his parents. He was groaning in his sleep.

After I introduced Mum she went into action checking Harold's pulse and feeling his forehead.

"May I?" She asked pointing to his tummy. Mum rubbed her hands to warm them, and then gently felt for where his pain was.

Harold whimpered loudly, "It make my cry."

"I can't be sure but I think it's his appendix. If it is, he needs an urgent operation," Mum said as she put a comforting arm around Harold's mother who was sobbing.

"But we can't go up. If he goes up we may all be found. What shall we do?" She sobbed. Mum thought for a minute.

"I'll take him. He's the same age as Jack – a bit smaller - but no one need know," Mum suggested.

Harold's parents whispered amongst themselves and eventually agreed: "Will you take him please? I will look after your children but please take him or he be sure to die here," his mum sobbed.

Sam would stay with Pip, I would go with Mum. Dad would look after Jack and make sure the baby sitter was gone before we got up to the house. Everyone cried as Mum left with Harold cradled in her arms, wrapped in a shawl and looking more like a doll than a child.

Mum rang a doctor friend of hers at the hospital and checked he would be on duty that night, whilst I held Harold. He was so light and frail; not chubby like Jack. She told the doctor that Harold was part of a traveller family who were being pursued by dangerous criminals so he needed the operation urgently and in secret. Amazingly he agreed to help. Mum said the doctor would lose his job if anyone found out but that he had helped people in similar situations before. Mum gently bathed Harold and dressed him in one of Jack's baby-gros and he slept all the way to the hospital, in Jack's car seat. He continued to sleep at the hospital, just whimpering occasionally.

It was appendicitis. Mum's friend sorted everything out and Harold had the operation straight away. Mum assisted, so I sat in an empty room for what seemed like forever waiting and thinking about the wonderful times we had had with our friends.

"He is a strong little chap; but his appendix had almost burst and would have poisoned him," the doctor announced, "I wish we could keep him in for a week or at least until he comes around."

"We can't," Mum said, "the people who are after the family are only a few hours away so they need to move fast." He gave Mum dressings and medicine so that Harold's family could look after him after his operation. Mum carefully smuggled him back to the car seat and I sat holding his hand as he slept all the way to our house.

Dad made a fuss when we got home but Harold's big eyes only opened enough for him to return a little smile, then he went straight back to sleep.

"Stella called by again," he told us. "She said Natalie has been in tears and won't tell her why. She said she will be here at eight o'clock tomorrow morning to talk with you. She kept asking about the cellar – she suspects something."

"Oh no! What shall we do?" Mum asked.

"Well, the builder's coming at seven-am with a lorry load of rubble to fill the cellar in, so you'd better get that little one home and our Sam back," Dad said.

"Can we stay down there a while Mum – to check Harold settles ok and to say goodbye?" I asked and Mum nodded.

Chapter 10

Goodbyes

We stayed with them until really late. Mum sat talking with their parents and checking Harold, whilst Hannah, Pip and Rebecca played with us. We explored all the tunnels again and even managed a midnight swim. As we sat by the pool we all made a wish. Hannah wished she could visit our house.

"Me too," Rebecca said.

Sam wished we could find a way to visit them – find another way to the tunnels.

"Me too," I said.

Pip nodded then said, "I wish I could kiss Kate!" And quickly kissed me on the cheek. We all laughed as I wiped it off with my towel.

"If I had known today would be our last time together I would have got you all a present to remember us by," I said.

"I know, let's meet in the den at six o'clock, before the builders come, and swap presents then," Sam suggested and it was agreed. We were all sleepy but didn't want to miss this last night of our adventure.

"When I be 16 I will make sure I be a runner and I will come to see ye," Pip announced.

"That would be great," Sam said, but for me that felt too far in the future.

Mum appeared at the pool. "Come on you two, it's time to say goodbye."

We all hugged and cried, and said goodbye. As we made our way up to the cellar my heart was beating as fast as the first time I came down those steps – not with fear this time but with sadness.

Sam set the alarm for half past five – only three hours away. Reluctantly I fell asleep and I jumped out of the bed when the alarm went off.

I put all my Barbie dolls in a bag. I knew Hannah would like them more than I ever did. I put hair braids and brushes in for Rebecca and three china dolls – I hoped Grandma wouldn't remember how many she had bought. I found some of Jack's toys and jigsaws for Harold.

There was no time to wrap them so I filled a huge Christmas gift bag each for them. Sam sleepily made a bag up for Pip with cars, action figures and a Frisbee.

I had two bracelets in a box. Each had one half of the same heart. I took one out and put it in my drawer and wrote 'To Pip from Kate' on the box with the other one in it. I wasn't keen on boys but Pip was a true friend and I would always remember him when I wore this bracelet.

We left a note on the kitchen table '6AM – GOING IN THE DEN – DON'T LET THE BUILDER IN UNTIL WE ARE OUT PLEASE!' We quickly made our way to the den with a bag of donuts and a bottle of lemonade, wondering if Pip and the girls would have managed to wake up in time. When I looked down the ladder I could see they were all sitting around our table with one of the torches on.

"Great!" Sam said. "We didn't know if you would make it."

"How is Harold?" I asked

"He be fine. He eaten four bread pieces already this morning – we will need another crop machine if he carries on like this!" Pip joked, and we all laughed with relief.

"We did bring you gifts," Hannah proudly said as she passed us a cloth bag which fit into my hand. "They be for all your family, for your new room and for that doctor who did save Harold's life."

I felt a little embarrassed as Sam brought the four *huge* bags down and even more so when I remembered the bracelet I had put in Pip's bag.

"I know, let's open them after we have parted. Then we don't waste this time together and we will have something to look forward to," I suggested and everyone agreed.

We talked about what we wanted to do when we grew up. Hannah wanted to be a teacher like her mum. Rebecca said she wanted to be a nurse like my Mum. Sam said he would like to be a policeman and we all laughed as he did an impression of chasing someone with a truncheon. I didn't know what I wanted to be but I did want it to involve adventures like the ones we had all had together. Pip went last and said, "All I want to be is a runner so I can come and see ye all," which made us sad again.

"Beep, beep, beep" – the builder's lorry was here. We needed to go. "Come on you two it's five past seven – we must get this filled in before Stella arrives", Dad shouted down the ladder. We huddled in a circle. We hugged and we cried again.

"Take care of ye now," Pip said as he went down the steps, followed by Hannah and Rebecca who had their heads down sobbing.

"Wait, your presents!" Sam said as he passed the big bags down the steps. My eyes were blurred with tears as I watched Dad and Sam put the slab over the steps. I ran up to my bedroom and cried even more. Sam followed me and I could see he was crying too.

"Oh no – stop the builder – I left their present to us on the table!" I remembered.

Sam put his arm up to stop me and pulled the cloth bag out of his pocket with his other hand: "Good job one of us is awake," he said. We could hear the rubble crackling in to our den. This was the end of our summer adventure.

I looked out of my window. George was at the door – it was only half past seven. His bike lay higgledy-piggledy on the drive with its wheels still spinning.

"Quick – you've got to stop her. She's on her way with a camera crew!" George gasped.

"Don't worry," Mum said. "Look – the second load of rubble has just arrived – so no one is going anywhere near the den."

I heard Stella's shrieks as she tried to get her camera crew to the cellars whilst Dad calmly told her it wasn't safe. She eventually went off with her hands in the air shouting at George as the crew loaded their cameras back into their car.

"That was close," Mum said as she appeared with drinks for us. "What have you got there?" She asked pointing to the cloth pouch on my bed.

"I don't know what it is yet. It's a present from the Tunnellers – for all of us but let's wait for Dad and we can open it together. I'm too tired now. " I suggested and passed the bag to Sam as I turned my face towards my pillow to hide my tears. Eventually I fell asleep crying. It was nearly teatime when I woke up from one of my many dreams in all of which I could hear Huw howling for me.

I wasn't at all hungry as we all sat around the table. The builder was gone until tomorrow. George and Nat were gone until next week. Our Tunneller friends had gone for what seemed like forever.

Sam put the time capsule on the table: "I thought we could bury this in the garden next week when Nat and George are back," he said. Then he dropped the cloth bag next to it. I had forgotten about both of these things.

As we all sat around the table I casually loosened the string on the bag. There were little pouches inside with each of our names on including one for Nat and George and one for the doctor. A larger pouch had a note on it; "*This be in thanks for your friendship to my family and our village. Do sell these to pay for your building – you should get a fair price.*" Dad and Mum opened the large pouch and what looked like ice fell out. I soon realised the seven pieces of ice were actually diamonds! Like the piles of ice I saw in the cave when I whizzed down the slide.

Sam's pouch had a red stone set in a small knife, Jack's had a red stone set in a dish and mine had a ruby ring in it. We peeped in Nat and George's bag to find they had a knife and a ring too but in pale blue stones. The doctor's bag had seven pieces of ice in it like Dad and Mum's. We all sat in silence. The gifts were amazing but I would swap them all for the chance to see our friends every day.

"*This is the part of the hidden treasure*!" I announced hardly able to believe my own eyes.

 "And the annoying thing is we can't tell anyone," Dad protested.

"This is too much!" Mum declared and we all agreed. Jack put his dish on his head and we all laughed. "Especially as they have already given us a gift for our family." Mum added as she went to the front door.

"What gift?" Sam asked

"Wait and see," Dad was smiling far too much – what could it be?

I could see our babysitter carrying what looked like a wriggly baby in a blanket.

"He's been crying all afternoon," she said before Mum took the bundle off her and walked back in to the kitchen.

"I know I said *never* but Pip's family have enough to do caring for Harold and the new baby at Christmas so we agreed with them that we would have him"

Mum announced - then I heard a little howl and I knew it was Huw!

"Huw!" Sam and I both shouted as I scooped him from the blanket. Sam rubbed his face in Huw's belly, Jack squealed, I cried and Huw licked my tears away.

"There's a note ... shall I read it?" Dad asked. I nodded through the tears.

"I do give my dog, Huw, to Kate, Sam and Jack for them to keep and love. Even though he be a useless hunting dog he is good for hugs and I know he will help you track me when I do become a runner in five years and we can all meet again. In friendship and love - Pip."

Dad sold all but one of the diamonds through different dealers and gave half the money to the local children's hospice. He also made a donation to our school to pay for all the children to go on a day trip to Nottingham Castle and the Caves after the school holidays.

That left enough money to pay for the extension and a week in a caravan at the seaside. We took George and Nat with us as Stella was going away with her new boyfriend from the paper shop.

The sun shone and Huw made it fun chasing the ball along the beach with his ears bouncing and his flag tail waving, falling into the sea in his excitement and then, too tired to walk back, sleeping in Jack's buggy with him. But we all agreed that nothing would ever match our time with the Tunnellers.

No one knew about my daydreams on the beach - as I played with my heart bracelet. Staring up at the cliff face I planned how I would train Huw to be a proper tracker dog and how I could learn to be a rock climber so I could climb the narrow crags and find Pip and our friends sooner. Maybe it was just a dream but stranger things had happened that summer.

Dad had the last diamond set in a ring for Mum and she wore it proudly every day. Mum put all our pieces in a safe at the bank and George and Nat agreed to theirs being kept safe too – until we were all adults. Dad got an allotment in the village, where he took us all to teach us how to grow vegetables and fruit.

The doctor donated most of the money from his diamonds to the children's hospice too but copying Dad's idea, he had one diamond put in to a ring and asked his girlfriend to marry him. We were all invited to their Christmas wedding.

By the end of the summer holidays the extension was built and Sam had moved into his new room. I was in my room daydreaming about our pool and the tunnels and caves. I laughed to myself about Larry and I thought about Pip, Rebecca and Hannah, and I wondered how Harold was.

Natalie and I had become good friends through our adventure. We decorated the Larry-mobile as a medieval cart for the village parade and dressed up as Robin Hood's men, including the bows and arrows Pip had given us, as part of our costumes.

We had already planned to do the next show and tell together on 'Family Pets' and had been to a couple of puppy classes with Huw so we had a few tracking tricks planned to show the class.

Any thoughts of wanting a big house went as we all realised how much we loved living in our cottage and how it connected us to our friends in the tunnels and to history. Mum loved her job as a nurse, but she did drop down to one night a week.

I snuggled up to Huw on my bed, sighed and turned my TV on just as the newsreader said: *"There are more crop circles appearing across Nottinghamshire and into Lincolnshire. Experts remain baffled. Some claim aliens are responsible; others say they are a hoax. The truth is they remain a mystery as no one really knows how crop circles are formed."*

"Oh yes they do!" I said and laughed out loud as Huw wagged his tail and licked my ears.

- - - - - - - - - THE END - - - - - - - - -

Note to the reader.

We are burying our time capsule with this story in it, at the bottom of our garden, in 1989. If you have just read this story then someone must have found the capsule and the secret is out – please think about how you can help protect The Tunnellers and the future of our country.

Stay in touch:

Writer - Helen

www.facebook.com/TheTunnellers

Artist - Kevin

www.KBArt.co.uk

Information about places mentioned in the book

Nottingham's 450 caves www.cityofcaves.com

Nottingham Castle
www.nottinghamcity.gov.uk/nottinghamcastle

Major Oak at Sherwood Forest Visitors' Centre & Abbey
at Rufford Abbey & Country Park
www.nottinghamshire.gov.uk

Undercover waterfall and tunnel at Newstead Abbey
Park www.newsteadabbey.org.uk

Sherwood Forest www.forestry.gov.uk.

Forest and hunting grounds at Clumber Park
www.nationaltrust.org.uk/clumber-park

Underground canal and bottomless pit at Speedwell
Cavern www.speedwellcavern.co.uk

Witch's cave at Treak Cliff Cavern
www.bluejohnstone.com

Wedding church, St Mary's Church Edwinstowe
www.achurchnearyou.com/edwinstowe-st-mary

Will Scarlett's grave, St Mary's Church, Blidworth
www.achurchnearyou.com/blidworth-st-mary

Local cave dwellers at www.ourmansfieldandarea.org.uk
and www.creswell-crags.org.uk

For more local history:

www.blidworthhistoricalsociety.co.uk

www.sherwoodforestvisitor.com

www.heritagebritain.com

www.nottinghamcavessurvey.org.uk

www.experiencenottinghamshire.com

Places to stay in Blidworth

www.blackbullblidworth.co.uk

www.hollylodgenotts.co.uk

www.redlionloft.co.uk